The Four Getters and Arf

Written by Helen Lester
Illustrated by Brian Karas

SNIFF

GoodYearBooks

The four Getters and Arf went on a picnic. "How nice it is to be together," they said.

"I forgot the eggs," said Brother
Getter. So he went home
to get the eggs.

Bye, Brother Getter.

"I forgot the sandwiches," said
Sister Getter. So she went home
to get the sandwiches.

Bye, Sister Getter.

"I forgot the drinks," said Daddy Getter. So Daddy Getter went home to get the drinks.

Bye, Daddy Getter.

"I forgot the fruit," said Mommy
   Getter. So Mommy Getter went home
   to get the fruit.

Bye, Mommy Getter.

"I forgot why I am here," said Arf.
So Arf went home.

Bye, Arf.

The four Getters and Arf had a picnic. "How nice it is to be together," they said.